e Ff Gg Hi

Nn Oo Pp Qq

Ww Xx Yy Zz

A is for Alden
—J.S.

To my three rascal friends—Grace, Lucy, and Georgia
—M.S.

THIS IS A BORZOI BOOK PUBLISHED BY ALFRED A. KNOPF

Text copyright © 2009 by Judy Sierra • Illustrations copyright © 2009 by Melissa Sweet

All rights reserved. Published in the United States by Alfred A. Knopf, an imprint of Random House Children's Books,
a division of Random House, Inc., New York.

Knopf, Borzoi Books, and the colophon are registered trademarks of Random House, Inc.

Visit us on the Web! www.randomhouse.com/kids

Educators and librarians, for a variety of teaching tools, visit us at www.randomhouse.com/teachers

Library of Congress Cataloging-in-Publication Data
Sierra, Judy.
The sleepy little alphabet : a bedtime story from Alphabet Town / by Judy Sierra ; [illustrations by Melissa Sweet]. — 1st ed.
p.   cm.
Summary: Sleepy letters of the alphabet get ready for bed.
ISBN 978-0-375-84002-9 (trade) — ISBN 978-0-375-94002-6 (lib. bdg.)
[1. Stories in rhyme. 2. Alphabet—Fiction. 3. Bedtime—Fiction.] I. Sweet, Melissa, ill. II. Title.
PZ8.3.S577Sle 2009   [E]—dc22   2008024526

MANUFACTURED IN CHINA
June 2009
10 9 8
First Edition

the sleepy little alphabet

A Bedtime Story from Alphabet Town

written by **judy sierra** • illustrated by **melissa sweet**

Alfred A. Knopf　New York

It's sleepytime in Alphabet Town.
As moms and dads run round and round,

the little letters skitter-scatter,
helter-skelter—what's the matter?

Uh-oh! **a** is wide awake.

And **b** still has a bath to take

with chubby **c**

and rub-a-dub **d**.

"Make room for me!" says eensy **e**.

f is full of fidgety wiggles.

g has got the googly giggles.

h tries standing on her head.

i and **j** jump on the bed.

k won't give a kiss good night.

l cries, "Don't turn off the light!"

m is mopey,

n is naughty.

Oops!

o and p upset the potty.

q is quiet as a bunny.

r and S read something funny.

t tucks in her teddy bear.

u takes off his underwear.

V is very, very snoozy.

W is wobbly-woozy.

X expects a great big hug.

y is a yawning cuddle bug.

Who's that snoring **Z z z**'s?

See you in the morning, abc's!

Aa Bb Cc Dd

Jj Kk Ll Mm

Rr Ss Tt Uu Vv